How Music Came to the World

An Ancient Mexican Myth

Retold by **Hal Ober**   Illustrated by **Carol Ober**

Houghton Mifflin Company   Boston   1994

For Emil, Betty, and Doris Ober
—H.O.

For Sylvia and Charles Schwab
—C.O.

Library of Congress Cataloging-in-Publication Data

Ober, Hal.
   How music came to the world / retold by Hal Ober ; illustrated by
Carol Ober.
      p.   cm.
   Summary: Retells a Mexican legend in which the sky god and the
wind god bring music from Sun's house to the Earth.
ISBN 0-395-67523-5
   1. Aztecs—Legends.   2. Aztecs—Religion and mythology—Juvenile
literature.   3. Music—Folklore.   [1. Aztecs—Legends.   2. Indians
of Mexico—Legends.   3. Music—Folklore.]   I. Ober, Carol, ill.
II. Title.
F1219.76.F65024   1994   93-11330
398.2′089′974—dc20   CIP
[E]   AC

Printed in Singapore

TWP   10   9   8   7   6   5   4   3   2   1

Author's Note

This book is a retelling of a Mexican myth that passed through many centuries of pre-Hispanic culture. I first came upon it in the book *Mexican and Central American Mythology,* by Irene Nicholson.

The source I mainly relied on is a poem reproduced in translation by Ms. Nicholson, from a sixteenth-century Nahua manuscript. My retelling closely follows that account but includes two modifications and some liberty in the dialogue.

First, the poem leaves to the reader's imagination what the House of the Sun looks like, so I have added a labyrinthine city for Quetzalcoatl (Kayt-zel-kó-ah-tl) to pass through before he hears the musicians.

Second, the poem suggests that it is the sky god, Tezcatlipoca (Tez-cat-lee-pó-kah), who explodes with rage at the disobedience of the Sun's musicians. I have chosen to attribute the outburst to his representative, Quetzalcoatl, to avoid any confusion caused by an abrupt reappearance of the sky god.

Finally, the dialogue between the two gods is a free interpretation that tries to be faithful to their often contentious partnership.

Illustrator's Note

The illustrations for this book grew out of my love for the imagery of Mexican mythology. To see those images in their natural setting, I made two trips to Mexico, visiting the ancient sites of Tenochtitlán, Malinalco, Tula, Teotihuacán, Mitla, Monte Albán, and Palenque. I photographed desert and jungle, sketched artifacts in the Museo Nacional de Antropología in Mexico City, and collected dozens of books containing pre-Columbian botanical and zoological motifs and the codices of the Aztecs and the Mayans.

Finally, I was fortunate to learn about pre-Hispanic music firsthand from the folkloric band 0.720 Aleación, based in Mexico City. Their style is a fusion of pre-Columbian and modern music played on ancient and modern Mexican instruments. The music inspired in my illustrations a similar fusion of motifs from many Mexican cultures and my own impressions.

My goal was to come as close as I could to the way a child might envision this ancient story. The scenes were not pre-planned but improvised. Moving the cutout oil pastel drawings around on a miniature stage set, I tried to infuse each scene with the intricate rhythms and harmonies that I found in the Mexican imagery and music.

One day two gods met on a wild and windy plain.

One was Tezcatlipoca, the sky god. The other was Quetzalcoatl,
the wind god. They were both very powerful. Sometimes they fought
each other. But sometimes, like this time, they helped each other.

Tezcatlipoca spoke first. "What took you so long?" he said.

"It's hurricane season," said Quetzalcoatl. "I've been busy. I've been whipping up the waves."

"This is more important than hurricanes!"

"I'll be the judge of that," said the wind god.

"Stop huffing for a moment and listen," said Tezcatlipoca. "What do you hear?"

Quetzalcoatl listened. "Nothing," he said.

"Exactly! Nothing! No one sings. No one plays a note. The only sound to be heard is the sound of your roaring. We need to wake up the world, Wind. And I don't mean with hurricanes. We need music!"

"Music?" said Quetzalcoatl. "What does that have to do with me? I have no music."

"I know," the sky god said, "but I'll tell you who does have it: the Sun. He surrounds himself with singers and music-makers who play and sing for him all day long, and he won't share their music with us."

"Won't share?" said Quetzalcoatl. "That's not fair."

"I know," said Tezcatlipoca. "So listen, Wind. I want you to travel to the House of the Sun. I want you to bring back the best singers and the best musicians. Remember," he said as the wind god unfolded his wings, "we need to wake up the world. We need music!"

Quetzalcoatl hurled himself into the air. He flew over land and
sea, searching the endless coastline for a single beach. He knew
there was only one way he could travel to the House of the Sun.

Spying the beach at last, he landed and called out the names of
the sky god's three servants: Cane and Conch, Water Woman, and
Water Monster. When they were all before him, he ordered them to
make a bridge.

The servants grabbed hold of each other. They began to grow tall
and thin and to twine together like a rope. They turned into a strong
rope bridge that disappeared into the sky.

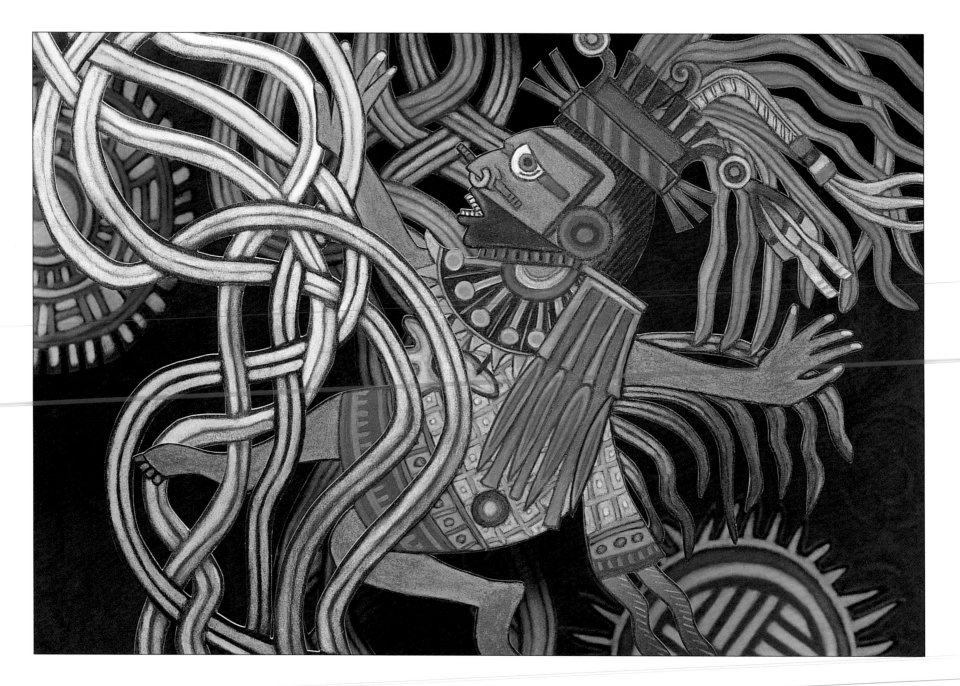

Quetzalcoatl climbed the bridge, following it higher and higher,
as the earth grew smaller and smaller below.

Finally he came to the House of the Sun. He could see its towers shimmering in the distance. Getting to them was not so easy, though.

He had to find his way through a maze of streets with high walls.
He kept getting lost and going around in circles.

Nearly ready to give up, he heard a beautiful sound that he had never heard before. It was cool and bright. It was sweet and light. It was music.

Quetzalcoatl followed the sound until it led him out of the maze.
Then he saw the musicians in the great courtyard of the Sun.

The flute players were dressed in golden yellow. The wandering minstrels wore blue.

The lullaby singers were dressed in white, and the singers of love
songs wore red.

Suddenly the Sun saw Quetzalcoatl. "Stop playing!" he cried.
"Stop singing! It's that terrible wind! Don't even speak to him, or
he will take you back to that silent planet of his!"

Quetzalcoatl lifted his wings and called, "Musicians! Come with me!"
None of them said a word.

Again the wind god cried out, "Singers! Musicians! The Lord of the Sky commands you!"

The musicians remained silent.

Quetzalcoatl did not like to be ignored. He exploded with anger, like a hundred hurricanes going off at once. Lightning cracked and thunder boomed and clouds swirled around the House of the Sun, turning the daylight into darkness.

The wind god roared as if there were no end to his voice. Everything
fell down. The Sun flickered like a tiny flame. The musicians ran to the
wind and huddled in his lap, trembling with fear.

Instantly the wind's anger passed. The thunder faded and the clouds
vanished. Quetzalcoatl took the musicians in his arms and left
the House of the Sun, moving through the maze as if it were not there.
   The wind god was filled with great happiness as he followed the sky
bridge back to earth. He felt like a father carrying his children home.

The earth could also feel that something new was coming—
something it needed and had been secretly wishing for. As the wind
god came nearer, the earth let out a slow sigh of relief. Its fruit began
to ripen and its flowers began to bloom with new, deeper colors.
The whole planet seemed to be waking up from a long sleep.

Finally Quetzalcoatl touched down on the earth with the musicians
and singers. They looked around curiously at the silent, waiting planet.
Then they began to play.

Through forests and valleys and deserts and oceans they wandered, filling the air with music.

Soon people learned to sing and play, and so did the trees and birds, the whales and wolves, the running streams, the crickets and frogs, and every other creature.

From dawn to dusk the melodies spread until music covered the earth.

The wind god was pleased. So was the sky god. The musicians
were happy with their new home.

And ever since that day, the earth has been filled with music.